Zorah
and the Very
Big Question

by **Deborah C. Mortimer**
Illustrated by **Stephanie Hider**

Library of Congress Control Number 2021903460

ISBN: 978-1-7366770-0-1 (Hardcover)
       978-1-7366770-1-8 (Paperback)
       978-1-7366770-2-5 (Ebook)

Front cover images by Stephanie Hider
Book design by Praise Z. Saflor

First Edition, 2021
Published in the United States by Leap Forward Publishing, LLC

**Leap Forward
Publishing** OVERCOMING CREATIVE HURDLES

www.leapforwardbooks.com

Dedicated to my beautiful nieces,
Naphtali, Kalleah, Aziza, Kailyn and Ariel.

Always remember, there is no limit
to what you can do!

Love always, Niecey

On Friday, Mrs. Robertson asked her first-grade class a very important question:

"What do you want to be when you grow up?"

Zorah looked around. Everyone's hand was up—everyone's but hers.

"I want to be a nurse, like my mother," said Sarah.
"I want to be a racecar driver," said Brandon.
"I want to be a pilot," said Kyle.

"What about you, Zorah?" Mrs. Robertson asked.
"What do you want to be when you grow up?"

Zorah just looked at her desk.

"I don't know," she whispered.

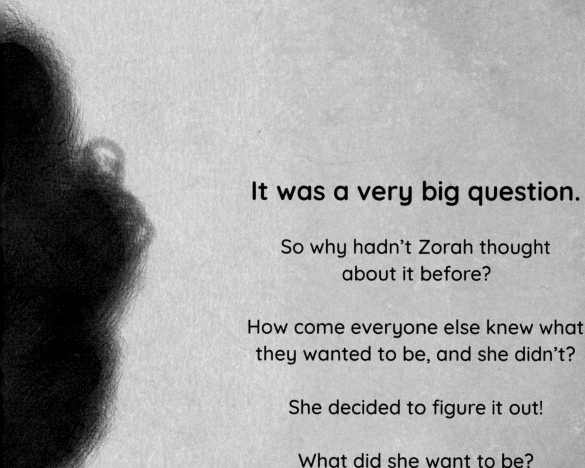

It was a very big question.

So why hadn't Zorah thought
about it before?

How come everyone else knew what
they wanted to be, and she didn't?

She decided to figure it out!

What did she want to be?
What **COULD** she be?

Zorah looked at Mrs. Robertson.
Her class was so much fun,
and she taught Zorah
new things every day.

Plus, whenever Zorah had a question,
Mrs. Robertson always listened and
answered her with a big smile.
She said Zorah
asked really
good questions.

Zorah thought about the time she'd
taught her dad how to make paper
butterflies. He'd said that Zorah was a great teacher
because she explained everything really well.

Maybe I can be a teacher,
  like Mrs. Robertson, Zorah thought.
     That sounded good,
          but what else could she be?

Zorah thought about it all day.
When the bell rang to go home,
her mom was outside waiting for her.

"Hi, sweetie," her mom said.
"What did you do at school today?"

"Mrs. Robertson asked us what we want
to be when we grow up," Zorah said.
"Everybody had an answer but me.

I don't even know
what my choices are!
How did you know what
you wanted to do?"

"Everyone's different," Zorah's mom said.
"I thought about the things I'm good at doing.
Why don't you try thinking about
what you like and what you're good at?
You make up great stories.
Maybe you can be a writer.
Or how about an astronaut or an astronomer?
You like looking at the moon and the stars."

Zorah was still thinking about her mom's words when they pulled up to her mom's office. Zorah often went there after school. Zorah's mom was a lawyer. She worked hard standing up for people's rights.

Zorah thought about her best friend, Dawn. Once, when they were playing a board game with their neighbor, Julian, Zorah stood up for Dawn's rights. Julian had wanted to take an extra turn, and Zorah told him that he wasn't being fair to Dawn because it was her turn.

Zorah's mom had said she was acting like Dawn's lawyer.

Standing up for Dawn felt good,
Zorah thought.
Maybe I can be a lawyer.

On her mom's desk, Zorah spied a picture of her favorite aunt.
Aunt Laila was a scientist. She was really smart.
She studied hard and did experiments to discover
new things and learn how things worked.

One time, she helped Zorah do an experiment
where they made their very own volcano EXPLODE!!
It was so much fun.

Maybe I can be a scientist like Aunt Laila, Zorah thought.

That night, after Zorah's dad helped her with her homework, he turned on the news.

"Daddy, why do you always watch this?" Zorah asked.

"Because news reporters tell us everything we need to know about what's going on in the world," he said.

Zorah thought about what her dad said.
She loved to tell her mom and dad about what she'd learned
at school and what was happening with her friends.

That's kind of like being a reporter, isn't it? she wondered.

NEWS

After dinner, Zorah's mom let her watch some TV before bed. Her mom explained that the people in her favorite show were actors.

"What are actors?" Zorah asked.

"They are people who use their imaginations and play pretend to tell us stories," Mom said.

That sounds like fun, Zorah thought.
When I play with my stuffed animals,
I pretend I'm an explorer going on
all kinds of adventures.

I guess that makes me kind of like an actor, too!

That night, Zorah fell asleep wondering about all the other things she could do.

On Saturday morning, Mom said, "Zorah, don't forget we have to go to the doctor for your checkup today."

Zorah liked her doctor. Dr. Ryan was nice, and when Zorah was sick she gave Zorah medicine to help her feel better.

Whenever Nana is sick, I help her take her medicine and bring her chicken soup to make her feel better, Zorah thought. Maybe I can be a doctor!

The next afternoon, Mom took Zorah on a special trip to the ballet. Zorah watched in awe as the head ballerina twirled and leaped in the air like a bird.

Zorah loved to dance in her bedroom. She liked to pretend she was a ballerina, putting on a show for her teddy, Mr. Fuzzy Face, and her other stuffed animals.

Zorah's mom pointed at the head ballerina. "If you go to ballet classes and **work really hard**, you could be a ballerina just like her," she said.

Zorah's mind was spinning. She had no idea there were so many jobs she could do!

That night at dinner, she talked with her parents about it.

Zorah's dad said she could be a chef like him or a police officer like her aunt Jasmine. Her mom said she could even be a strong athlete, like her favorite tennis player— **if she practiced hard enough**.

Later, Zorah watched TV with her parents.
A woman came on to give a speech.

"Pay attention, Zorah," her mom said.
"This woman is very important."

"Why?" Zorah asked.

"Because," her mom said,
"she's the **vice president of the United States**.
Maybe she can help you answer your **big question**."

Zorah listened to the woman. She said that she wanted
little girls who look like her to know that if they worked hard,
they could be anything—**even vice president or president!**

Zorah couldn't believe it.
**The woman on TV did look like her,
and she was vice president!**

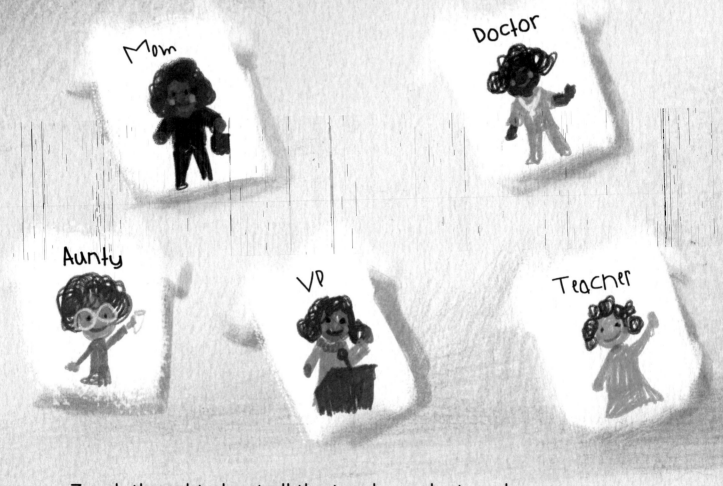

Zorah thought about all the teachers, doctors, lawyers, and other career people she'd seen and learned about. Some of the people who did those jobs were **smart, strong, brave women**. They all worked really hard, and some of them looked just like her, too!

The vice president on TV was right!

On Monday, Zorah couldn't wait to go to school!
She ran right up to Mrs. Robertson.

"I don't know what I want to be when I grow up yet, but I do
know what I **CAN** be!" she said.

"That's great, Zorah,"
Mrs. Robertson said.
"What's that?"

Zorah smiled a big smile and shouted,

"Anything I want!"

What do you want to be when you grown up?